The Pumpkin Patch

Halloween Madness - Book 1

A Starlight Investigation Short Story

Marnie Atwell

ISBN: 978-0-6450281-3-3

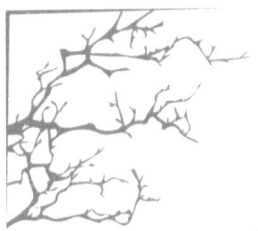

Chapter One

Briella searched everywhere for the pouch that held Scout's special pencils. An image of the perfect costumes for Halloween had popped into her head, and she wanted to get them down on paper before she forgot them. No matter where she looked, she couldn't find it. Briella was beginning to think that Scout had hidden the pencils on purpose, from her.

With a great deal of frustration, she gave up her search and grabbed a lead pencil that lay beside a phone on the bench in the kitchenette. Excitement over her project had the creation of fairy dust in full production. Smiling from ear to ear, she sprinkled a little dust from her fingers and watched as the pencil shrank to a more manageable size.

Briella picked up the implement after tearing a piece of paper from the message pad and flew to a rectangular coffee table in the living area. She placed the paper on the surface, then lay on top and began to sketch.

She drew for over half an hour, being careful to get the shading right. Regularly flying to the ceiling to ensure the proportions were right. The picture was incredibly detailed which would make it easier for April to replicate with material once Briella gave it to her.

She was lost in her own thoughts when April and Scout came in with a surprise. She scooped up the paper and folded it a few times before shoving it beneath a glass container shaped like a leaf.

April placed a large object covered with a pillowcase in front of her. "I've brought you a surprise," she said with a smile.

"What is it?" Briella asked.

"Pull the fabric off and have a look," April chuckled.

Briella did and was thrilled to be staring at her wardrobe. She had been living out of her suitcase for the past week, and while that was all well and good, sometimes her mood dictated she wore an outfit she hadn't thought to pack.

Briella flew over to April and gave her a big kiss on the cheek. "Thank you so much," she smiled, fluttering in front of her with hands clasped together.

Briella travelled back to her favourite piece of furniture and opened the doors. A battery operated sensor light affixed to the ceiling came on, illuminating the racks of clothes for Briella's selection. Her eyes were like stars twinkling in space. Scout stood beside her dumbfounded. "Briella, I've got to say, you take an obsession for fashion to new heights."

"Awww thanks, Scout," Briella laughed, threading an arm through her friend's, bent at the hip.

"I know you don't bother fussing over clothes. Let me just say, before the week is over, I will have you wearing a completely different outfit to your usual purple shirt and black pants."

"No, you won't," Scout said a little smugly.

"Yes. I *will*. And I'll tell you something else, you are going to love it," she grinned, bringing out the dimples in her cheeks. Scout's eyes skimmed over her friend's body. She knew she would never feel comfortable in an outfit of Briella's choosing.

Her latest makeover included changing her hair to a gorgeous ebony with bright red highlights. It was probably one of her more toned down looks. A few days ago, her hair had been fluorescent green.

She wore a full-length, sleeveless jumpsuit in red and black print. The outfit was matched with a pair of silver heels with red straps that wrapped around her feet. Briella's makeup consisted of a dark grey smoky-eye, rose-beige coloured cheeks and lips that were coated with a deep-red gloss. She was beautiful to behold and wore her look with the confidence of a supermodel.

'There is no way I could pull that look off,' Scout thought to herself. "Nope, not going to happen," she replied to Briella's question, feeling quite comfortable in her own attire.

4

THE PUMPKIN PATCH

"Baby steps, Scout. I will wear you down with baby steps," Briella smirked, peering into Scout's purple irises while lifting a handful of short, purple strands of hair. "Have you ever thought of getting hair extensions?" Briella cackled with laughter as Scout batted her hand away. "Will you stop it?"

"Never. Bwahahaha!"

April burst into laughter herself reminding the fairies they had company. "My apologies for our rudeness, April," Scout said sincerely.

"You have nothing to be sorry about, Scout. Friends are supposed to get lost in the joy of being together. What are your plans for the day?" April inquired.

"I'd like to check out the landscape around the property you are buying with Force before you return to the city with Briella. I'm a bit hesitant to look around an unfamiliar place on my own. Briella, will you come with me?"

"Love to."

"Sounds very sensible. Would you like me to stock your satchel with goodies?" April asked.

"That would be wonderful," Scout beamed.

"I'll get right on it. How long are you planning to be gone?"

"Just a few hours, I should think," she turned to Briella to gauge her thoughts.

"Sounds good to me," she responded.

"Right. Where do you keep the satchel?" April asked.

"On top of the fridge," Scout replied. One of April's eyebrows shot up into the air. Scout thought that was quite clever, making a note to try it herself the next time she was in front of a mirror. "Force tends to knock it onto the ground if I leave it anywhere else."

"Understood," April nodded, stepping towards the kitchenette.

"Speaking of Force, where is he?"

April answered over her shoulder, "He's stepped out for the morning."

"That's not an answer," Briella frowned. "What's he up to?"

"Nothing."

THE PUMPKIN PATCH

"Then why won't you tell us where he is?" Briella stamped her foot.

"Because it is none of your business," April stated, stepping up to the fridge, hoping Briella would let it drop, but knowing she wouldn't. She turned around to find Briella hovering at eye level, glaring at her.

"I'm not leaving until you tell me where he is."

"That's fine, Briella," April moved to one of the lower cupboards and opened the door. She pulled out a brown paper bag from the top shelf. "You can stay here all day, but that might upset Scout."

She opened the bag and took out a couple of small mushrooms before replacing the bag in the cupboard. April tucked them safely in Scout's satchel and turned her attention back to Briella's face. "Scout needs your help to find the safer spots on the property and to discover what level of danger exists there."

"Then tell us what I want to know, and we'll be off."

"She's not going to tell us, Briella. Leave it be."

"But…"

"It's fine, Briella. Grab the satchel from April so we can get going. Thank you for the snack, April. All going well, we'll be back for lunch."

"Take care out there, girls. Force and I should have thought to investigate the area for you both."

"Don't sweat it. I've already been all over these hills when I was hunting down the Jealousy Monsters. Though, I'd had more important things on my mind than my own safety. It's a bit different this time, flitting around thinking about becoming a creature's next meal."

"If you want to wait, Force and I could come with you this afternoon."

"Nah. We are fairies, not sissies. We've got magic and all that," Briella waved her hand in the air dismissively. "We'll be fine."

Briella snatched the satchel from April's hand and turned her back on her. Scout shook her head with disappointment. It didn't take much to alter her friend's mood from grateful to nasty.

THE PUMPKIN PATCH

She followed Briella through to the living room and waited for April to open the window. It was early in the morning, and the pub wouldn't open for hours yet. Even so, it wasn't worth the risk of a human spotting them by using the standard means of entering and exiting the building.

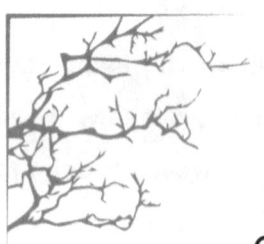

Chapter Two

"**C**an you believe her, Scout?" Briella's lilac irises were still covered with a thick emerald filter. Scout opened her mouth to remind her she had forgotten to change her contact lenses to colours that matched her outfit but changed her mind. She figured there was no need to upset her further.

"Don't trouble yourself over it, Briella. Force will tell me all about his escapades later when we are alone."

"And what if he doesn't?" she turned her head looking left then right. "Where are we going?"

"Fly north," Scout directed. "He always tells me things."

"But what if he doesn't?" she asked, checking the location of the sun before changing direction.

"Then we'll have something else to occupy our time with, won't we."

"You mean spy on him."

"Absolutely," Scout affirmed with a sneaky grin.

"Ooh, it is so nice to be able to spend time with you, Scout. I hope we don't pick up any creature vibes for a couple of weeks."

"Won't you be bored by then?"

"Not even. You do know Halloween is less than two weeks away, don't you?"

"Is it?"

"Good Lord, Scout. Lucky I am here to help you get prepared. I'm surprised Force hasn't mentioned it to you. It is our busiest time of the year after all."

"Hmmm," Scout murmured thoughtfully. She wondered if his absence had anything to do with the upcoming event. Brushing that thought away, she looked around, taking in her surroundings.

Scout delighted in the feeling of freedom that came from being outdoors in the less populated areas of the country. She revelled in the freshness of the air that was breathed into her lungs. "Isn't it wonderful?" she asked, falling into a controlled spiral through the atmosphere.

Briella screwed up her face a little. She wasn't used to being in that sort of environment. Her flights had involved darting between buildings that were only a few metres apart from one another.

The enormity of the change in lifestyle that this move would bring suddenly became clearer, impacting on her psyche. Her chest tightened and her breathing hitched in her throat. Her arms flew to her throat as she gasped for air.

"I don't think I can do this," Briella gasped with terror on her face.

"Down there," Scout pointed to the ground, recognising the tension in Briella's body. Briella was being plagued by a panic attack. Something Scout had experienced many times over the last three thousand years on Earth. She supported Briella through her awkward landing, laying her gently on the softly, cushioned grass.

"You are going to be okay, Briella. Concentrate on your breathing. In and out, nice and slow." Scout kept constant eye contact. She didn't give Briella an opportunity to break the connection thereby ensuring she was only concentrating on the simple task of breathing.

"That's it, Briella. You are doing great," Scout's calm voice caressed Briella's taut nerves.

"I don't think I can move to this town, Scout," Briella gulped. "There is too much emptiness here. Nowhere to hide."

"Sure, it is a bit bare in this part, but just wait until we get to the forest. If it is anything like my home in the hinterlands, you are going to love it."

"It is too far away. Maybe we should wait until Force and April can take us to the tree line."

"Yeah, we can do that," Scout murmured, gently tucking a few strands behind Briella's ear.

"Are you mad at me, Scout?"

"No, of course not. Do you think you can get to your feet? We should probably make our way back to the pub."

"Yes. I'm okay now," Briella said, rising slowly. They retraced their flight path to discover they were locked out of the room. Knocking on the window had no effect. April couldn't hear their tiny taps. "Should we throw something at the window?"

"No, I've got a better idea. Follow me."

The excitement in Scout's voice had Briella brimming with anticipation. She stayed in Scout's slipstream, conserving energy for later. Scout took them to the back of the pub where renters could keep their cars under cover.

It was early in the storm season which ran from late September through to early April. So far that October, the weather had wrought havoc on six occasions and they were only halfway through the month. Briella spotted April's car, and her eyes lit up like a Christmas tree. "Great idea, Scout," she giggled, knowing precisely what Scout had in mind.

They arrived at the driver's window to find that April had remembered to leave it down a smidge. She did this in case they found themselves in trouble and needed somewhere safe to go. Scout flew in first, then fluttered down to the lever that would open the boot. "I hope it's still in there," she gritted her teeth and pulled with all her might.

"Why don't you use your magic?" Briella asked, flying down to help her.

"I don't want April getting the fairy dust all over her fingers next time she needs to fill up the tank."

"Point taken," Briella huffed, nearly flipping backwards when the lever finally gave up its fight and complied with their wishes. "It's open," she cried, racing Scout for the exit. Briella got there first, leaving Scout to wait patiently for her turn to leave.

Briella flew around the back of the vehicle and attempted to raise the lid of the boot on her own. Scout howled with laughter. "If we could barely manage the lever to open the darned thing, how do you think you are going to lift that heavy piece of metal?"

"A girl can try, can't she?" Briella's hands had found her hips. Her hostile attitude was beginning to rear its ugly head again.

"Do you think you could find something we can wedge underneath for some leverage?"

"What are you two up to?" April's voice came out of the blue, scaring them half to death.

"We are trying to get in there," Scout pointed.

"Why?" April asked.

"Transportation," Briella announced.

"Nah, uh," April stated emphatically.

"Yes," Briella returned forcefully.

'Oh boy,' Scout thought. "Can we talk about this, April?"

"No, Scout. This is not up for discussion."

"What if you were in control of the vehicle and we were merely passengers? We could call you when we are ready to return. You could come and collect us in person if that would make you feel better?"

"Did you even remember to grab your phone?" April asked with uncertainty.

"Yes," Scout tapped the device attached to her ear. "So, can you please do this for us? It would be way more fun than you carrying us on your person."

THE PUMPKIN PATCH

April felt the tugging of her heartstrings as she gazed into Scout's eyes, imploring her to say 'yes'. She gripped the lid of the boot and lifted it swiftly. Before she could stop them, the fairies had flown into the vacant space in front of her and gazed lovingly at her pride and joy.

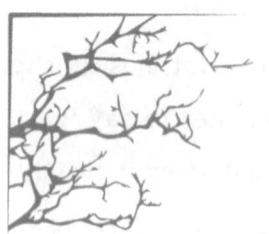

Chapter Three

April reached around the fairies, "Come on, out of the way." She placed her hands beneath the box and lifted it carefully from the confines of the car. Setting it gently on the ground, she took great care while removing the item from its packaging.

"It is so beautiful, April. Where did you get it?"

"It was custom made by a dear friend of mine. You know if you had tried to get it out yourselves you would have damaged it, and I would've had to skin you both alive as punishment."

"Awww, you're just saying that because Halloween is just around the corner."

"That would've been your punishment regardless of the time of year, Briella."

"Did you know that Force hadn't even warned Scout so she could prepare?"

"Why would he need to tell you?" she gazed at Scout with confused eyes. "Shouldn't you be able to feel the coming of All Hallow's Eve?"

"My system is still out of whack from my stint on the coast. The sand doesn't do me any favours, and it takes weeks for my senses to come right again."

April appeared sceptical, "Wouldn't you still have known roughly how many weeks out it was before you headed to the beach?"

"It messes with all sorts of things, which is why I try to take on as many jobs as I can in the country. Unfortunately, the creatures quite often prey on the city kids, probably due to the higher number of bodies in a smaller space."

April flicked a few switches on the device then grabbed the controls. "Well, are you going to get into the helicopter or not?"

"Yay," they cried, opening the door and climbing into the command centre. Where the outside of the vehicle had been a shiny silver and blue, the inside was luxuriously decked out in fawn coloured leather. The seatbelts were hastily put on and, with a thumbs up at April, they were soon lifting up into the air.

Despite April's reluctance to let the fairies use her baby, she had the biggest smile plastered across her face. Scout's phone began ringing. It was April, "Do not get out of the helicopter until I have put it on the ground safely and given you permission to leave. I will fly the chopper back to me when you are clear of the rotors and collect you in person when you are ready to come home. Any questions? Good. Please relay this information to Briella and make sure she follows my instructions or this will be the last time you ever get a ride. Comprehend me?"

"Yes, ma'am."

During her conversation with Scout, April had turned them towards the tree line they were travelling to earlier. She walked behind the helicopter, checking for obstacles that might cause it to crash. She skillfully navigated it around the building and monitored the airspace between them and the forest.

THE PUMPKIN PATCH

There were many benefits to being a Gatherer. The most useful in this situation was the ability to modify her eyes to be able to see long distances clearly. From what she could see, there were no creatures currently occupying the airspace that posed a danger to her helicopter.

The girls were pleased that a person had created something so fun to ride in. They wondered if the humans who rode in adequately sized helicopters felt the same way they did at that moment. It was a strange feeling to be moving through the air without the use of their wings.

Another thing that was strange to them was the feeling of security that enveloped them. They could see butcher birds and silvereyes flying in the distance but were not in fear of being hunted for food. Briella could gain an appreciation for the beauty of their surroundings without being paralysed by fear.

It wouldn't be good if Briella decided to hide away in the forest rather than make a dash from the house to the woods. Worse yet, she could choose not to move there at all. She was an extrovert who required a lot of attention, more than Scout could provide on her own. For this to work, Briella needed to become comfortable with all aspects of country living.

Briella seemed quite comfortable in her seat. Her breathing was calm, and she was leaning as far forward as the seatbelt would allow. She wanted to view as much as she could through the windscreen, and panels of glass on the door. They didn't have headsets to be able to talk to one another. Everything that was going through her head would have to wait until they landed.

The ride was long, though quite a bit shorter than if they had flown under their own steam. Not having access to a watch or clock, Scout wasn't sure exactly how much time had passed. At a guess, she would say it had taken about fifteen minutes. They landed roughly five metres from the tree line. Close enough to duck into the brush safely in case of attack, but far enough away for April to operate the machine without incident.

April rang Scout's phone and provided more instructions. The fairies exited the vehicle and flew a metre from the blades of the chopper. Scout indicated they were safe then watched the helicopter rise into the air, turn around and zoom back to its owner. Scout noticed Briella jumping up and down excitedly. "Don't do that," she admonished. "You look like a grasshopper begging to be eaten."

"Maybe a few days ago when my hair, wings and outfit were green," Briella brushed the back of her right hand over her body.

"You still look like a grasshopper the way you are bouncing around in the long grass."

"Oh," she peered around worriedly.

"You'll be fine. You need to take precautions out here just like you do at your place in the city."

"Different predators out here, though."

"Not really," Scout explained as they flew for cover. "There are birds, lizards, and snakes which you already have in the city. Then there are possums, echidnas, Brown Antechinus and Fawnfooted Melomys which are similar in looks to rats and mice, wallabies, bats, flying foxes and bandicoots. Some of which you would have spotted in the city."

"I've seen a possum before, and plenty of rats and mice in the city at times. There is a large colony of flying foxes that passes over our apartment at dusk. I can't say I've seen any of the other mammals, though. Are they very dangerous?"

"Sure, if you are stupid enough to put yourself in front of them."

"I should have changed my outfit," Briella stated as she gazed into the distance.

"Do you have adventure clothes?" Scout questioned, pretty sure the answer would be no.

"No," Briella sighed, "but I do have a darker jumpsuit that might have blended better than this red one."

"Why don't you design some when we get back to the pub? From the looks of it, April must be nearly finished with your house, or she wouldn't have retrieved your wardrobe. She is going to have plenty of time on her hands, and we don't want her going stir crazy with boredom."

"I'll think about it," Briella replied, striding off into the woods.

"Wait up, Briella."

"What for?"

"We're not here to explore the forest."

"We're not?"

"No, most of the animals that live here will be asleep until nightfall. I wanted an opportunity to talk to you without April dipping into our brains with her mind-link abilities."

"What for?"

"I want to plan a Halloween surprise for Force and April."

"I'm in."

"You haven't even heard my ideas yet."

"Doesn't matter. It is going to be epic," Briella said, rubbing her hands together.

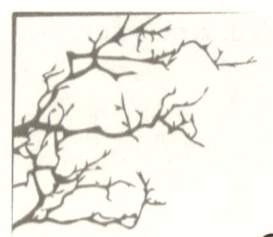

Chapter Four

Scout and Briella flew to a rock the size of a loaf of bread and got comfortable. It was half in shade, providing the perfect choice for a fairy who liked the heat and a fairy who liked the cool.

Briella stretched her legs before her and leaned back on her arms. She tipped her head towards the sky and basked in the sunlight. "If we stay here too long, I am going to need to find something to drink."

Scout sat facing Briella with crossed legs, her forearms supported by her thighs. "There's quite a few daisy bushes just over the rise with plenty of flowers in bloom."

"Oh," Briella gasped, leaning forward and pointing a finger in Scout's direction. "You've been here before, you lying devil."

"Speaking of devils, I'd like to organise a Halloween party for Force and April. What do you think would be better, making props to place in the house when settlement takes place or creating a spooky forest?"

"Definitely the forest. That way we can begin now, and it won't be such a rush to get it done in just a few days. Also, being in the forest, they will have no idea we are planning a surprise *if* we can keep them out of there until All Hallow's Eve."

"That's what I thought," Scout said, nodding her head.

"What happens if the portal to the underworld begins to open in our territory?"

"Don't worry about that, Briella. By my calculations, which Sophia at Starlight Investigations has double checked for me, the most logical locations based on the alignment of the planets this year are the land masses along the Atlantic Ocean in the Northern Hemisphere. We are ninety-nine percent certain Australia won't be affected, which leaves us open to having some fun with fake monsters for a change."

"Yeah, the Americans seem to enjoy this time of the year with tricks and treats. It's catching on here, too. April and I had lots of humans in costume knocking on our door last year. I should imagine there will be even more this year."

"Don't count on anything too much here, Briella. These kids live a lot further apart than the children in the city."

"Then we will have to organise a party. You are in charge of creating and delivering the invitations. Shouldn't be hard seeing as though you know where a lot of these kids live. I will take on the design and creation of our outfits," she grinned. Her job was already done.

"How are you going to do that without April getting suspicious?"

"She makes us a costume every year. I will tell her we will have a quiet party to help you become less rigid in the way you dress and your routines. I will tell her I need her help in encouraging you to take baby steps. She will be falling over herself to help you enjoy life more."

"Who says I don't enjoy life a lot, now?"

"We are getting off task," Briella waved her hands in the air. "We can work out the nitty-gritty later. What sort of props do you want in the forest?"

THE PUMPKIN PATCH

Scout closed her eyes and pictured the scene she had envisioned in her mind when Briella had pointed out All Hallow's Eve was near. She explained the images to Briella as she saw them.

Sticky, spider silk hanging from branches in clumps, catching unsuspecting wanderers by surprise. Ghouls which had motion sensors attached to them appearing out of thin air, tearing screams of terror from the toughest child and adult alike. The sound of their outcries would cause skeletons to ascend from trap doors built into the ground as though they were rising from the dead.

Wireless speakers attached to scattered trees creating a level of tension throughout the forest. Lanterns lit by flaming candles hung at eye level providing ambient lighting.

Bubbling cauldrons with cackling witches standing over them placed strategically throughout the woods with no possible way to go around them. The revellers would have to fight their way through or backtrack to find another route.

"That sounds fantastic, Scout. Is it like a maze?"

"I don't know. I guess it could be."

"What else did you see?"

"Scarecrows with scary faces chasing people around. Zombies attempting to catch people so they can eat their brains. A headless horseman, gnomes, trolls, vampires, and werewolves running amok."

Briella's face was glowing with delight. "We could make it a condition of coming that the townspeople wear a costume from a list we give them. They could then be given a role based on the costume they chose for part of the night."

"What do you mean?" Scout asked intrigued. She thought Briella could draw them and they could use their magic to bring them to a 3D state. They wouldn't be able to move, but the fright factor would still be there.

"Say some partygoers came as zombies, then between seven and seven-thirty they would have to round up as many people as they could to eat later. We could make a pen of sorts for those who are captured to wait in until the next time slot began. The captured could then be released for the next monster to catch between seven-thirty and eight."

"That is a wonderful idea, Briella."

THE PUMPKIN PATCH

"How are we going to get all of this organised in the next ten days?"

"Piece of cake. That is what magic is for."

"But my magic is always wonky at this time of year. Isn't yours?"

"I haven't had any problems so far. What usually happens? Maybe we can work out a way to lessen the negatives."

"It's different each year."

"So what hasn't happened so far?"

"It's a bit hard to tell, isn't it? You don't always know what can happen until it does. I haven't died yet."

"Has anyone else?" Scout asked, her voice dripping with alarm.

"Not yet," Briella shrugged. "There's always a first time, right?"

"Not this year," Scout shuddered.

"How can you be so sure?"

"You're with me," she said in a matter of fact tone.

Briella burst into laughter, reading between the lines. What Scout hadn't said was, 'As if anything could go wrong with me there."

31

"So what type of monster are you thinking of emulating?"

"Maybe something cute like a black cat. I haven't done one of them in a while.

"So what are you thinking of dressing me up as?"

"Well, cats are quite often considered to be familiars."

"You want to dress me up like a witch?"

"A pretty witch, like Samantha Stevens or Glinda. Not like the wicked witch of the west."

Scout pouted. "Are you thirsty yet?"

"Yeah, I could do with a drink."

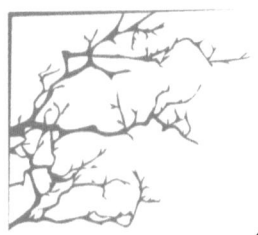

Chapter Five

Scout fumed all the way to the daisy bushes. Of all the costumes for Briella to suggest, that was the one that hurt her the most. Scout wondered if that was how Briella thought of her, as an evil, fun-sucking witch. She had never met a helpful witch, nor had she sought one out.

Her speciality lay in picking up vibes from creatures who wanted to hurt children. No witch that was good was ever going to give off those sorts of signals. Hence the only witches Scout had ever knowingly come into contact with was of the evil kind.

The logical part of her brain told her she was thinking ridiculously. The insecure part of her mind was saying that her friend didn't like her much, but she didn't have any other fairies to hang with, so she made do.

Scout felt her mood plummeting. Rather than allow the tension to build between them, Scout decided to tackle her feelings head-on. "Do you really see me as a witch?"

"What sort of a question is that?" Briella glanced over with furrowed brows.

"A genuine one," Scout replied, holding her friends gaze.

"I don't understand why you would associate my costume choice with how I see you as a fairy."

"Then why did you suggest a witch's costume?"

"You are the most powerful fairy on Earth. What with my magic going wonky at this time of the year, it made perfect sense for you to be the witch and me the familiar."

"You want to dress as a pair?"

"Well duh. Seeing as though we can't mix with anyone at the party, I thought it would be fun to pretend we were in cahoots with one another. Us against the world."

Scout looped her arm through Briella's. "I am so sorry I misunderstood your reasoning. I think I need to work on my self-esteem."

"No, you don't. You just need more practice with being around others. You have lived on your own for a long time. Never having to second guess yourself. Now that you have others around, you are probably worrying, constantly, about what we think of you. In time, you will learn not to care. Until then, we will just have to love you the way you are, uncertainty and all."

"Thanks, Briella," Scout leaned her head against Briella's.

"Now that that's out the way, let's drink." They grabbed a couple of flowers each and sucked the sweet nectar. "What do you think we should begin with? I was thinking of making some spidery silk stuff and draping them over branches. They will look natural enough if we can make it appear like Spanish Moss."

Scout squeezed her eyes closed then opened them quickly again. She repeated the process a few times.

"What's wrong?" Briella jumped to her feet.

"Something's up with that tree. Is your magic doing that?" Scout pointed to a spot over Briella's shoulder.

"No, I haven't used any magic here." Briella turned around and stepped back in fright. The tree was bulging, as though it was giving birth to something. After a minute or so, the outline of a body appeared. A few seconds later, the impression of a face began forming. "Wow, Scout. We have a wood nymph living in our forest."

"That's impossible. They've been on the extinct list for the past five hundred years."

"Well, how do you explain that?"

The texture of the growth began to change. The irregularity of the paper-bark started to flatten, becoming smoother. The colour transformed from grey to cream. The bark framing the face which had become quite defined turned a reddish-brown.

The eyes of the creature pried themselves open revealing iridescent irises in an ocean green. The more delicate details of her body took shape; the mouth, ears, nose, fingers, and toes.

The nymph peeled herself from the tree. She was only a metre tall, but her presence made her seem larger than life. She was so beautiful it almost hurt to look at her. If Scout and Briella hadn't witnessed her transformation, they would have assumed she was an angel.

She glared at them with blazing eyes. Scout and Briella huddled together. From the look on the creature's face, she did not come bearing good news.

"Why are you threatening our forest?" the nymph asked with a huskiness to her voice.

"I beg your pardon!" Scout shouted.

"Answer me now, or be obliterated."

Scout flew towards the nymph but was batted away before she could reach the creature's ear. *'How am I supposed to talk to you, if you won't let me near your ear?'* she thought as she tumbled through the air at a dizzying speed before she righted herself.

About to try again, she paused when the creature shrunk to their size. Scout landed beside Briella, being careful to ensure her actions appeared peaceful. "We have not come to threaten your forest," Briella assured her, glancing at Scout as she joined them.

"We have come to drink some nectar from the daisy bush," Scout chimed in.

37

"I sense there is great danger here, and the source is emanating from the two of you."

"We will not bring harm to your woods."

"We may not," Scout replied thoughtfully, "but the humans might."

"Don't be ridiculous," Briella said. "How are they going to hurt the forest?"

"They could swing off branches and break them, they might bring chainsaws and pretend to be that scary guy in the movie. There are a lot of ways the trees and creatures could get hurt if we hold a Halloween party here."

"That will not be tolerated," the forest deity stated. "You may not gather in these woods with humans."

"But they are not dangerous," Scout countered. "We hunt monsters that are far worse than humans."

"I am saddened to hear that, young fairy. The humans are the most dangerous creatures on the planet. But they will fade into the background soon enough."

"What does that mean?"

"Can you not feel it?" she asked.

"What?" Briella countered.

"The purge is nearly upon us," the nymph's gaze seemed to burn through to their soul.

"How long do we have?" Briella panicked.

"A decade, maybe two," the nymph shrugged.

"Plenty of time to throw a party and grab a new outfit then."

"Seriously, Briella. Can we throw a party on the flat land between the house over there and the edge here?"

"You can do whatever you wish outside of the forest. Be warned, if harm comes to my children by your hands, you will live to regret your decision."

"We will make sure your forest remains pristine."

"Thank you, fairies. Now if you'll excuse me." She grew to her natural size and pressed herself against the flesh of the tree. Slowly, she began to reintegrate herself.

"Wait, we don't even know your name!" Scout shouted, before realising the nymph couldn't hear her.

She fluttered closer to the creature, waiting for an arm to come up and flick her away. It never came. She flew to the nymph's ear. "What is your name?"

"Dynopiah," the creature replied.

"Will we see you again?"

"Perhaps."

Her face lost its definition, and her unblemished skin became rough and grey. Within minutes, all evidence of the creature's existence had disappeared. The tree appeared exactly as it had before Dynopiah made her presence known.

Scout looked at Briella and said, "This has been an incredible day. Are you ready to go?"

"I think so," Briella nodded. "Are you going to call, April?"

"Yes. Unless you would like to fly home." Briella shook her head. "I didn't think so." Scout made arrangements with April. "Come on, Briella. Let's get back to the drop-off zone. She will collect us from there."

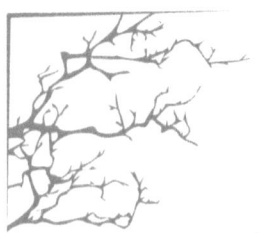

Chapter Six

Scout and Briella picked some daisy blossoms and placed them in the satchel in case they got thirsty on the journey back. Briella broke off a piece of mushroom and began munching on it as they walked to the pickup zone. Scout decided to join her once the smell of the flesh penetrated her nasal passages.

The forest was quiet, peaceful. Most of the animals that lived in the area were sound asleep. Every now and then they heard some rustling in the leaf litter. The fairies paused in their tracks and peered around intently. Once they had determined they were safe, they resumed their journey, treading carefully. Soon the sounds were forgotten, and they were talking and laughing together, once more.

The vegetation was similar to the rainforest where Scout had lived previously. The bottlebrush trees were in bloom; their fluffy red flowers providing sustenance to the parrots that flew harmlessly above them.

The grevilleas were also in flower. Their spidery apricot blooms attracting insects that in turn brought in the jenny wrens, one of the smaller species of birds which appeared harmlessly cute, but were deadly to the unsuspecting fairy. Scout eyed them cautiously, still hoping to tame one someday. She longed to pat one but knew how dangerous that would be, especially when they were teaching their young to hunt.

Scout was beginning to feel quite cold. She usually packed a light jacket when she went on trips. The excitement of living with Briella had disrupted a lot of her usual routines, and Scout had left it back at the pub. She glanced at the canopy to see if the sky was visible, but it was completely hidden from view. "Does it feel stormy to you, Briella?"

THE PUMPKIN PATCH

"Now that you mention it, there does seem to be a bit of static in the air. I thought the temperature had been dropping for the last half hour or so, but when you didn't say anything, I believed I had imagined it."

"Perhaps we had better take a look." They flapped their wings, closing in on the edge of the woods within a few minutes. The flying got tougher, the nearer they got to their destination. No longer able to make headway against the wind, they landed and used the debris littering the forest floor as shields. The view from the tree line was frightening. "Uh, oh."

"You can say that again. What are we going to do, Scout?"

"Well, we are not going to panic," she replied, staring at the swirling mass of hail ladened clouds from behind the safety of a fallen log. The wind howled above them, its squall sending chills down their spines. Lightning flashed across the sky and arced towards the ground. Thunder rumbled, the ground vibrating beneath their feet.

"Can we make it to the pub before it starts raining?" They had great difficulty making it to the edge of the forest with the force of the wind blowing in their direction. How were they supposed to fly across the meadows? Scout ignored the stupidity of her question and answered it as though it was a natural thing to say in this kind of situation.

"I think it would be safer for us to head back into the forest and find somewhere above ground to take cover."

"Good idea," Briella said, looking at the scene before her. She turned around, stopping when a glint of metal caught her eye. "Look at that!"

The fairies pressed against the wind, sliding sideways as they stepped from behind a windbreak, struggling to stay on their feet. Making it to the next branch lying on the ground, they ran towards the object that had caught their eye. A remote-controlled jeep. It was a four-door, khaki-green gift from the gods, or more than likely, from April. They looked for a note, but there was none. Probably blown away in the storm.

THE PUMPKIN PATCH

The windows in the front doors had been punched out. The reason made clear when they tried to open the doors to find them glued shut. Peering in through the opening, they could see a shrunken version of a controller sitting on the dash. "Do you think it works?" Briella asked.

"I don't think it would be in this condition if it were a broken toy," Scout answered, taking another look at the sky. "Do you think we can make it?"

Lightning hit a nearby tree, the flash of light blinding them momentarily. The clap of thunder was immediate, the force of the soundwaves knocking them off their feet.

A large branch was severed from the trunk, falling swiftly to the ground. Both the broken limb and tree were sizzling, smoke rising slowly towards the sky. "I don't know, but I'd sure like to try. It is definitely not safe staying under these trees," Briella screamed.

Scout and Briella jumped to their feet, diving into the nearest window. Briella entered first, climbing over the centre console and landing awkwardly in the passenger seat. Scout quickly followed, holding her hand out to Briella for the controls after freeing her right-wing that had become trapped beneath her.

"Why can't I drive?"

"Two reasons. Number one, it's not a Ferrari or a horse, so you have no experience with the way it handles. Number two, I doubt you have ever driven over this type of terrain."

"No, but it can't be that hard."

"Do you want to bet your life on it? Because if you spin the wheels and get us bogged, we are going to be in all kinds of trouble."

The first blobs of rain hit the windshield. Briella scowled as she handed over the controls. "And how many times have you ever driven one of these?"

"Force and I had a couple of these when they first came out," she explained, pressing the power button. Scout gently pushed the accelerator with her left hand while she thumbed the steering lever with her right. The jeep lurched forward then gained traction.

Scout was quite proficient in her ability to control the vehicle. She was also pleased to see that this model had a working windshield wiper. It flicked backwards and forwards as fast as it could, but still, their vision was limited.

"We used to go to the park when it was storming and fling them around in the mud. The humans avoided being outside during lightning storms, so we never got caught. I used to beat him nine times out of ten," she stated smugly.

A piece of hail the size of a golf ball landed in front of their vehicle. Scout managed to avoid hitting it by millimetres. She closed her mouth and concentrated on getting them home safely. Hail began to hammer the earth, a thick band running the length of the meadow to their right. "We are going to have to take a detour," Scout yelled above the noise. "The storm is driving us towards Force and April's new place."

"That's good, though, right? If we can make it there, we can drive right underneath and wait it out. No damage to us or the vehicle."

"That's what I'm hoping." Scout veered left. Somehow they managed to stay ahead of the more significant pieces of hail. The smaller pieces hit the roof and sides of their vehicle. A couple even landed in Scout's lap, no doubt leaving a bruise. She shivered harder than she did before. Her pants becoming soaked in the time it took Briella to notice the hail on her lap and flick them out the window. Scout never took her eyes off the destination. She relied on Briella to guide the way.

"We are not going to make it, Scout. Head further to the left. There appears to be a makeshift shelter that might provide some protection."

"Hang on to the bar above your door." Scout veered around a hailstone the size of a tennis ball.

"Are you serious? I've been hanging on for grim life since the car started moving."

"You gotta admit, it's loads of fun, though. Even considering the storm."

"I'll let you know when my stomach is no longer in my throat."

"I hope the roof's not made of shade-cloth," Scout said as she drove undercover. "What the hell are those?" Scout shrieked at the same time that Briella shouted, "Look out!"

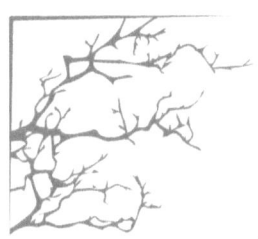

Chapter Seven

"Looks like we are in a pumpkin patch," Briella squinted through the windscreen. She not only had hold of the bar above the door, but she'd also leaned forward to grip the bar located above the glove box with her other hand.

Scout did a great job of dodging the giant obstacles, bringing them into the middle of the sheltered area. "I wish I'd packed a jacket," she shivered, manoeuvring the car, so it was hidden behind one of the pumpkins, protecting them from the wind.

"Did you know this was here? Before today, I mean?" Briella asked.

"No. I've only explored the forest area. I wanted to wait until the property belonged to Force and April before exploring the more open regions. I didn't want to chance being seen before the security measures were put in place to ensure the secrecy of our existence."

"You mean the crystals."

"Yeah. Force wants to have a discussion regarding the location of our new fairy garden. Until we have decided where we want to locate our home, he is reluctant to place the crystals."

"That's understandable," Briella replied, nodding her head. "Don't they weaken each time they are moved?"

"Yes, they become less effective. Do you want to get out and stretch your legs? We should be okay from the wind as long as we stay behind this pumpkin."

"That sounds like a great idea."

Scout turned the power off on the controller and lay the device on the dash. She climbed back out the window, a feat that was harder than her entry had been, she discovered. It seemed that Briella felt the same way. "Scout, I'm stuck!"

"Hang on a second," she cried over the noise of the hail still pelting the earth. Scout raced around the back of the vehicle and up to the front passenger window, grabbing hold of Briella's hands.

THE PUMPKIN PATCH

"Where's your other leg?" she queried, gazing speculatively at Briella's left foot.

"Tucked underneath me," Briella informed her.

"This isn't going to work. Can you get everything back inside?"

"Maybe."

Scout helped Briella get her arms, leg, and head inside the car safely. "Okay, change your position so that you are kneeling, facing me. Good. Now push your arms and head through the window. When I grab you by the armpits and pull, push off with your feet and tuck your wings in."

"Ooh," Briella's nose crinkled around the edges.

"Oh, for Heaven's sake, Briella. You don't have to touch them."

"But how could you think to do such a thing?"

"Do you want to get out of the car or not?"

"Yes," she pouted.

"Then follow instructions, and let me worry about your smelly underarms."

In no time, Briella was freed, and shaking off the images of Scout's hands on her armpits. Scout shook her head, "You are so weird sometimes, Briella."

"Wow, Scout. Lucky I don't have self-esteem issues. Those remarks would have had you worrying over how others viewed you," Briella commented with a flick of her head. Scout noticed the hair that Briella had spent ages straightening that morning was beginning to curl with the moisture in the air.

"You're right. I'm sorry." Scout said, following Briella's movement towards the pumpkin and watching her run her hand over its skin. The texture was rougher than Briella had expected. "Who do you think planted these? The Gatherers or the previous owner."

"They look a bit big to have been planted by April and Force. I guess the previous owners grew them."

"April and Force could've helped them become this big in a week."

"Yes, they could have. But they wouldn't want the locals to question things that don't have a logical explanation."

"Well, what about our fairy garden? How are they going to explain that away?"

Scout almost burst into laughter until she realised her friend was serious. 'How could Briella not know this?' she asked herself. "The locals won't be able to see our fairy garden, Briella, nor will they be able to cross the border of crystals."

"Won't they think a black spot in the middle of the landscape is a bit strange? Not to mention the fact that they won't be able to continue ahead when travelling in a straight line?"

Scout was incredulous, "Where do you live, Briella?"

"With April," she frowned, not understanding the question.

"Yes," she replied, waving Briella's comment aside. "Whereabouts exactly?"

"In my house."

Scout sighed, "Where is your house located, Briella? In a garden? Between a pair of stumps? On the balcony of April's apartment?"

"In the living room, on a coffee table," she answered.

"What happens when people come over?"

"They don't."

"How do you get your moonlight?"

"There is a palm tree in a terracotta pot on the balcony that I nestle in to soak up the rays."

"Where do you bathe?"

"In a bathtub." The look she gave Scout was insulting.

"What bathtub?"

"The one April ordered for me off the Internet."

"I don't understand," Scout shook her head with dismay. "Don't you wash yourself in a shallow stream, like me?"

"No, I certainly do not! There is a website that April orders all of my furniture through. I think they are designed for children's dollhouses, but they are perfectly sized for me," Briella clarified. "She bought me a bathtub, a container that holds water for bathing, from there."

"How does the water get in there?"

"April fills it up and empties it again when I am finished."

"How does she get it in and out of your house?"

"The roof is hinged."

"How big is your house, Briella?"

"There are twenty rooms in my house, but April said the new house is going to have two levels. Isn't that exciting?"

"What would you need two levels for?"

"I was hoping you would share it with me. The new house is going to have its own plumbing. April has been tinkering around with it for the past couple of days and believes she has got all the mechanisms in working order. She has bought a small, solar pump that is going to be attached to the collection tank. We can use the grey water to hose the plants in our garden."

"Are you planning on locating the house in the fairy garden?" Scout asked.

"Only if you want to live there, too. If not, I will ask April to find somewhere in her bedroom to put it."

Scout gazed at her friend, flabbergasted. The ancient fairy had not been living a fairy's life for what sounded like a very long time. The fact that she was considering not residing under April's roof when they moved was huge.

Scout welcomed the weight of responsibility that washed over her. She had the opportunity to reintroduce Briella to the wonders and benefits of being a fairy.

"I'd be happy to move into the new house with you," Scout said as she grasped her friend's hand

and squeezed. Briella grinned back, breathing a sigh of relief. She hadn't realised she had been holding her breath until the tension left her body.

Scout glanced back at the pumpkin that Briella was leaning against. "Do you think they grew them to eat, or for Halloween props?"

"I don't know," Briella said. "They'd make great jack-o-lanterns, don't you think?"

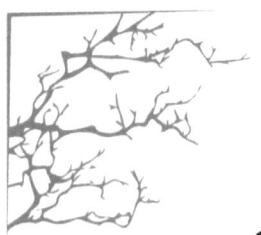

Chapter Eight

"Jack-o-lanterns?" Scout laughed, the word sounded preposterous to her ears.

"Where have you been hiding all these years?" It was Briella's turn to show her amazement at Scout's lack of knowledge.

"You grab a pumpkin, like this baby," she said tapping it, "and carve out a circle in the top. This becomes the lid. Oh, and don't forget to cut it on an angle. You don't want it to fall in when you put it back on. Then you carve out a face because it is easier to do this when the flesh is still inside. Once you are happy with your efforts, you scoop out the insides, put in a candle then light it, and replace the lid. There is your jack-o-lantern. Rinse and repeat."

"Oh, that's what they're called. I've seen them around the place. How do you know how to make them? I've only seen plastic ones hanging on people's front porches."

"There's a family that lives in our apartment building who don't have a lot of money outside of living expenses. The kids never miss out on anything because whatever the parents can't afford to buy, they try to make themselves. They create all sorts of decorations, and each year their stash continues to get bigger. I watch them while they create stuff on their balcony. That is where they do all the messy stuff, like carving pumpkins, glueing glitter and painting things."

Scout was beginning to realise that living with April had not stunted Briella as much as she had believed. In fact, it seemed that residing with April had exposed Briella to experiences that had broadened her view of the world.

Would living with Scout hinder that component of Briella's development or expand her own? Only time would tell. She looked at the few pumpkins that were visible to them at ground level.

"It's a shame Dynopiah won't let us hold a party in her forest."

"Yeah," Briella followed Scout's gaze. "The forest would have looked really spooky with all of those hanging from the branches of its trees."

"The atmosphere would have been unforgettable," Scout agreed. "Maybe we could set something up on our land."

"Like what? We've already decided a few days isn't enough time to create something incredible."

"It doesn't have to be mind-blowing. The townsfolk won't be disappointed if we don't have a lot of stuff this year. Once we gain access, we could mark out an area with a few posts to form a border. We could string some rope between them, tying two knots maybe a few centimetres apart to hang each lantern between. That way the lanterns won't slide around, damaging each other or cause the string to dip. Then we could decorate the area inside with the stuff we were talking about earlier."

"It won't be the same, though."

"No, but I'm sure Force and April will have a great time anyway."

"How are we going to fix the posts without their help?"

"We are fairies, Briella. We'll use magic." Briella worried at her bottom lip with her two front teeth. "Is something wrong?"

"No," Briella answered a little too quickly. She continued speaking before Scout would have a chance to remember that her magic went a little haywire at this time of year. "Will we carve the pumpkins the same way?"

Scout nodded her head. "We could save a load of time and money if you drew the props and we used our magic to make them become 3D."

"Oh, Lord," Briella muttered under her breath.

"Sorry, I missed that," Scout said.

"Nothing, it's all good. Hey, I think it's stopped hailing."

Scout flew carefully to the top of the pumpkin and poked her head above. She was pleased to discover the wind had died down. It was still blowing, but not as strongly as it had before. She called Briella up for a peek.

"Looks like the worst of the storm is nearly over. We should be able to head home soon, though the rain might hang around a little longer. We won't know for sure until the wind drops further and we can get a look at the sky."

Briella shrugged her shoulders. "I'm not in any hurry to get going. It still looks pretty dark out there."

"We might come across some water-courses that require a detour along the way," Scout muttered more to herself than to Briella.

"I don't know why humans call it the flatlands. When you are the size we are, it's an awfully bumpy ride."

Scout roared with laughter. "I am glad you are here, Briella."

"Me too," she grinned. "Watch this." Briella fluttered a little lower then, with a burst of energy, thrust herself above the pumpkin. She flapped furiously against the wind then turned her body to the side, allowing the breeze to sweep her away. Scout heard her whoops of delight before she soared out of range.

As Briella passed the next pumpkin on the vine, she dipped below the wind's reach and flew back to Scout, low to the ground. Scout flew down to meet her, admiring the blush that had spread across her cheeks. "That was so much fun, Scout. You should try it."

"I don't know," she said shaking her head. "I don't think I would enjoy not feeling in control."

"You won't know unless you try it. And if you find that you didn't like it, you don't have to do it again. I'll come with you if it will make you feel better about giving it a go."

Scout thought long and hard about whether she wanted to attempt this or not. She considered the things that Briella had learnt by putting herself out there among the humans. That must have been frightening for her at first, but then Briella realised she could do it safely, without being discovered.

She was still going through her 'do I' or 'don't I' reasons when she noticed Briella had given up on her making a decision. She was preparing to go herself again before the wind died down completely. Scout opened her mouth before her brain caught up and said, "Come with me."

Briella didn't give her any more time to think about it. She grabbed her by the hand and flew two-thirds of the way up the side of the pumpkin. "Fly fast, and when I say now, let go of my hand, twist your body and let the wind take you. I will be right beside you in case you get into trouble. Ready, go fast."

They flapped their wings with everything they had, and when Briella gave the word, Scout followed her instructions to the letter, feeling both terrified and exhilarated at the same time.

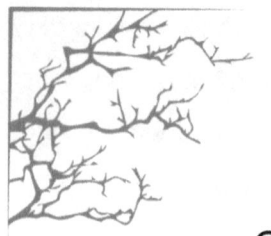

Chapter Nine

It wasn't until it was all over that Scout realised what a rush letting go could be. Her cheeks were flushed with colour, and her eyes sparkled with happiness.

She flew over to Briella and gave her a big hug. Briella was thrilled to see Scout appearing so childlike. "Do you want to go again?" she queried, already knowing the answer.

"Yes." Scout didn't wait any longer than it took to answer before riding the breeze again. She discovered there was just as much wind pressure above this pumpkin as there had been over the first one. She was surprised by that fact.

Scout decided to launch an investigation, testing the wind shear above all of the pumpkins between the other end of the shelter and herself. Only then would she be able to conclude with any validity whether the experience would lessen the further in they travelled.

She passed on her idea to Briella who indicated she was up for checking that theory. They got to the fourth pumpkin when Scout's phone began to ring. It was April.

She had been trying to contact them since the beginning of the storm to see if they were safe from the weather. While Scout talked to her, Briella waited on top of a pumpkin that was being blocked from the wind by another.

Unable to contain her happiness, Briella began to dance. She swayed to a rhythm of her own creation, her movements becoming more intense as the beat inside her head started to change.

She became lost in her own world, her eyes closing as she was swept away by a tide of strong emotions. Her brain no longer accepted messages from her body, which was trying to let her know what was happening in the environment around her.

The only thing her mind registered was the endorphins and fairy dust that was flowing through her veins while she danced. So it was a great shock when, after calling to her a few times, Scout threw a pebble which hit her on the shoulder.

Her eyes flew open, and her body jerked as a scream burned through her throat. Fairy dust burst from her pores, coating the pumpkin with golden speckles.

"You scared me!" Briella yelled once she'd managed to suck in a breath.

"I called you several times," Scout responded angrily.

"Sorry, I didn't hear you. I kind of got caught up in the moment," an impish grin spread across her face as she let go of her fear.

Scout huffed. She had lost the euphoric feeling from earlier. It wasn't as easy for her to let go of her anger as it was for Briella to flick off her fear. "The storm has passed, and the rain is steady. I think we should head back to the pub."

"Fine," Briella peered longingly at the pumpkins they hadn't gotten to. 'If only April hadn't rung,' she thought.

They flew back to the jeep in silence. Scout stewed over her decision to peg a pebble instead of drifting closer to her friend and repeatedly calling her name. Briella remained quiet due to the uncomfortable vibes oozing from Scout.

It was easier climbing into the vehicle this time around. Scout picked up the controller and turned it on. She looked through the windscreen, ready to start the wheels moving when she changed her mind. Scout rotated her arm to the left, bringing the device closer to Briella. "Would you like to take us home?"

Briella didn't know what to say. While she was touched that Scout had offered her an olive branch, the environmental conditions were poor for someone who had no experience with operating such a vehicle. She gulped down the fear of upsetting her friend and said, "Maybe you should drive us home."

Scout looked crestfallen. It seemed she had taken Briella's words as a rejection of her apology. To show Scout her intent had been complimentary, she said, "With the amount of rain we have had, I'm likely to put this baby on her roof. When the ground has dried, you might take me out for a lesson in cross country driving."

Scout grinned, "The locals call it four-wheel driving. I'll make you a deal." Briella's body took on a defensive posture. "I'll teach you how to drive the jeep if you teach me how to ride your horse."

"Which one? The animal kind or the five-hundred-and-fifty-plus horsepower kind?" Briella queried.

"Not the Ferrari. I already know how to drive one of those," Scout scoffed.

"In your dreams," Briella snorted, settling into the seat properly. "You have a deal. How come you have never ridden a horse?"

"How would a tiny horse in the woods be explained away?"

"A mini-miniature pony?" Briella giggled.

"Now you are just being silly." Scout roared through the pumpkin patch, spinning the wheels in a couple of places where the rainwater had run down the hill and into their sheltered area.

"If you are going to be nasty, then the deal is off."

Scout delved down into a simmering mood. Briella gave herself a mental slap to the forehead. 'When am I going to learn to keep my mouth shut?' She kept her watery gaze averted from prying eyes.

THE PUMPKIN PATCH

There was no need to show Scout how emotional she had become. The pumpkins whizzed by and were soon out of sight.

They were travelling in the same direction as the detour they had taken earlier. Briella assumed that Scout had finally decided to take a quick look at the piece of land they were about to inhabit. When the weather was more favourable, she knew they would venture out and map the area, identifying the perfect place to position their fairy garden.

There were some raised gardens that they couldn't see properly from their vantage point. From the trellises that were planted in the middle of them and the green leafy plants that adorned them, she figured they were some kind of climbing vegetables.

The part Briella found most interesting was the cornfields. Long spindly plants with huge ears of corn hanging from them like a giant alien sucking the life out of its host. A shiver wracked her body as tiny bumps appeared on her skin.

"Are you cold?" Scout asked, seeing the movement in her peripheral vision.

"I'm fine," Briella answered, keeping a wary eye on the plants.

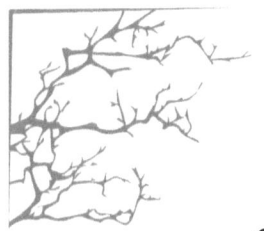

Chapter Ten

The building was on Scout's side, still a fair distance away. From this angle, it looked more like a cottage than a house.

Briella was sure that April and Force would enjoy living there once they had completed the renovations they had planned. That was if April could manage to live happily in the country like she hoped.

She'd never been able to stay there for long in the past, preferring the hustle and bustle of a large city and the sound of the surf at night to put her to sleep. That is, the few hours a week she managed to get some shuteye.

The attraction of the city for April was the night-life. There was always something to do or people to talk to in the wee hours of the morning that didn't occur in other areas.

Out in the country, most people were sound asleep during those hours when April was looking for something to occupy her time and mind. Those that weren't asleep were at their place of work or travelling to or from. They were no help to April at all.

Briella sighed, even though tensions were running high between her and Scout, she hoped April would stay there often. While she was considering moving into a home of her own, separate to April for the first time in centuries, she knew that if April left, she would go with her.

Briella wasn't quite ready to grasp total independence. Neither was she prepared to live with Scout full-time without a buffer of some kind. Since Force was Scout's best friend, there was nobody Briella could turn to if things went belly up between the two fairies.

Scout's voice broke into her musings. "We should be back at the pub in about an hour. Do you mind if we stop so I can have some nectar?"

"No, go ahead," Briella grabbed Scout's satchel and opened it. She took out two daisy blossoms, one for each of them. "You don't mind if I join you?"

"Not at all," Scout replied, bringing the car to a stop. "Are there any mushrooms left?"

"Lots. Would you like some?"

"Yes, please." The jeep was facing a paddock. The house was behind them to the right. "I wonder if the previous owners had any horses."

"Why are you thinking that?"

"Farmers don't usually have wooden fences unless there are horses, do they?"

"Don't think so. I've heard that wooden fences are more expensive than barbed wire but safer for the horses."

"I hope there aren't any in there."

"Are you scared of them, Scout?"

"Not really. I wouldn't like to try to outrun one in this, though."

Briella gazed at the interior. "Not exactly sturdy stuff is it?"

"No," Scout replied, feeling the dint of the roof from a hailstone lightly scraping against her head.

"I guess we should try our hand at panel beating when we get home."

Scout smiled. That was the first time Briella had called the pub home. Something she had yet to do. "We could try our hand at it. If it doesn't work, we can always use fairy dust."

The smile dropped on Briella's face for a split second before she put it back in place. "Yeah, magic fixes everything," she said, continuing the rest of the sentence in her head, 'Except at *Halloween when your name is Briella.*'

Scout drove under the bottom rung of the fence and flicked the accelerator to full throttle. She wanted to get to the other side of the paddock as quickly as possible, but there really wasn't any need. The farm animals that lived there had been gone for well over ten years, and the Australian natives that utilised the area were still in hiding from the storm.

The fairies made good time, reaching the pub in forty minutes. Scout drove around the back and found the bay that held the pale blue Cadillac. With an abundance of confidence, she threw it into reverse and made it all the way to the end safely, the bumper lining up with the radiator of April's car above. "Girl, you've got mad skills," Briella squealed, very impressed.

"Thanks. You going to be okay to get out or do you need a hand?"

"I would like to say I'll be fine, but I'm not sure I will," she grimaced.

Scout grabbed her satchel after turning the power off and placed the console carefully on the dash. Then she exited the vehicle with the grace of a ballet dancer and made her way around to Briella's side. "The same way you exited last time."

"Okay." Briella placed her arms and head through the window then wriggled forward enough for Scout to grip her armpits. She waited for Scout's assistance, showing her appreciation by not making any derogatory comments or pulling faces.

Once she was out, Briella ran her hands down the front of her abdomen. It was a little sore from being dragged across the metal until her wings could carry her weight. "Do you want to have a go at fixing the car now?" Briella rubbed a finger along her bottom lip as she considered the difficulties that would pose being parked in its current position.

"Nah, we'll come down and have a look at it later. Let's go inside to see if the Gatherers have returned."

"Do you think Force will be here?"

"I hope so. I'd like to know what he's been up to."

They flew up to the window they had used earlier. It was closed up tight. "Hurry before our wings get too waterlogged to fly," Briella cried, positioning her hands across her forehead to keep the raindrops off her face. Scout closed her eyes and concentrated for a few seconds before opening them and flicking her finger at the window.

Fairy dust flew from the tip and landed on the window frame. She wriggled her finger towards herself, feeling completely satisfied as the window opened at her command.

Scout flew inside and was immediately assaulted. "Don't come in here, Briella," she yelled, holding her hands up in front of her face to protect herself.

"I can't stay out here," Briella cried as the rain continued to pelt her delicate features. She followed Scout inside, horrified by the scene playing out in front of her.

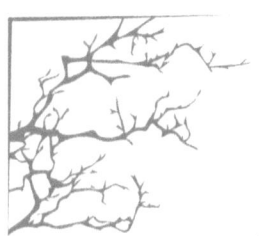

Chapter Eleven

Scout was being smacked across her body by a pencil. Of course, it was not just any old writing implement. It was the one Briella had shrunk earlier to draw their Halloween costumes with.

Briella raced into the room and gripped the fairy beater with both hands, wrestling with the beast in an attempt to take its attention away from Scout. It worked. The pencil's interest shifted to concentrate solely on her.

"Oh my God, Scout!" she screamed as it chased her around the room, hitting her anywhere and everywhere it could.

"Did you do this, Briella?"

"Yes, but not on purpose. It's never happened this early before."

"What hasn't?"

"The wonky magic. It usually starts a couple of days before Halloween, not ten."

Scout raced to the kitchenette. She grabbed the handle of the cage she had been kept in by the Jealousy Monsters which was located on the counter near the microwave. Scout had been furious with Force when he had brought it home with him.

Now she was incredibly grateful for the contraption. A sprinkle of fairy dust made it light enough for her to fly with. She flew to the coffee table and set it on top. Scout opened the door and demanded Briella fly inside.

"I'm not going in there," she cried, copping a whack to the face. "Oh," she whimpered, tears springing to her eyes.

"You don't need to stay in there. Just fly in, wait for the pencil to follow you then fly out. I'll slam the door shut and it will be stuck in there."

"Don't be ridiculous," her wings nowhere near fast enough to escape the pencil's brutality. "It can slide out between the bars."

THE PUMPKIN PATCH

"The cage nullifies magic, Briella. Once it's in there, it will be as dormant as it was before you dusted it," Scout yelled, chasing after them both, unable to intercept either. "I forgot you were quicker than me," she grumbled.

"You got my back, Scout?"

"Always, Briella."

Briella flew down to the coffee table and inside the cage, gripping the bars at the back so tightly her knuckles turned white. She squeezed her eyes shut as tightly as she could manage, and waited for a jab from the pointy end of the pencil. Nothing happened.

Briella let go of the bars with her left hand and spun around to face her offender. It lay motionless on the floor of the enclosure. "It worked," she whooped with delight, then checked her body for marks. There were quite a few.

"Has this happened before?" Scout asked as she helped Briella exit.

Briella cupped the side of her face with her hand, "Yeah, afraid so."

"When?"

"A few years ago. Any inanimate object my dust touched suddenly came to life. It only lasted until the following sunrise though, regardless of what time the object was infected."

They looked around the room. The pencil had been busy. There were scribblings all over the walls and ceiling. "I guess I'll be busy cleaning this up for quite a while."

"Don't be silly. Four hands are better than two and we'll have it cleaned up in half the time."

Scout flew to the kitchenette and plugged the sink. She ran some warm water then retrieved two sponges from the cupboard beneath the basin. She turned the tap off before the sink was deep enough to take a swim. Adding some detergent, she gave the water a swirl.

"How long until your magic goes back to normal?" Scout asked, shrinking the sponges to fairy size.

"The sunrise after Halloween."

"Okay. You are not to use your fairy dust until then," Scout stated in an authoritative tone. "Any magic that is required will be done by me."

"Oh," Briella moaned, flying for the window.

"What's the matter?"

"No, no, no, no," she muttered as she disappeared from Scout's sight.

Scout glanced around the room, then threw the sponges into the water. There would be plenty of time to clean up the mess once she had found out what was wrong with Briella.

"Briella!" By the time Scout arrived outside, she was nowhere to be seen. "Damn it, Briella. Where are you?" Scout flew around to the front of the pub and looked out over the landscape for a creature that looked like a butterfly. There was no movement in the area to catch her eye.

Scout tapped her foot in thin air, her wings flapping furiously to hold her still, while she battled to remain suspended in a downpour that attempted to ground her. If she didn't come up with an idea soon, she wouldn't be able to follow.

81

Scout shook her head at her own stupidity and zoomed towards the carport. Briella would have gone for the jeep. That was the only way she was going to get around quickly and safely in this weather.

'Thank God I reverse parked,' she thought, flying as swiftly as she could. She was just in time to see the jeep appear from under the car and zoom around the corner. 'Damn, *she's good.*' Scout thought with a touch of jealousy.

Slowly, her body came closer to the ground until with great reluctance, she placed her feet on the ground. Scout had only managed to travel a few metres before her wings had become too wet to fly.

She looked to the heavens and cursed them for her predicament, knowing that she had decided to follow Briella despite the dangers the weather presented. Scout walked with head down and wings tucked in. She probably should have turned around, but couldn't bring herself to abandon her friend.

She wished she knew what had caused Briella to take off the way she had. At the rate she was going, it would be hours before she found her. She put another task on her to-do-list. Organise a mobile phone for Briella. Preferably one like her own that tucked neatly into her ear, leaving both arms free to complete tasks. Then she would always be able to check to make sure Briella was safe, providing she answered the call.

Worried more about the welfare of her friend than her own stupidity, she pressed her finger to her phone and said, "Dial Force."

Instead of hearing Force's voice, she heard, "The number you have dialled is out of service. Please try again later."

With no idea where to begin looking for Briella, she turned around and walked back to the pub. Scout continued her attempts to contact Force, knowing sooner or later, service would return to the area.

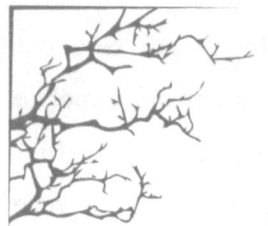

Chapter Twelve

Briella tore up the terrain on her way back to the pumpkin patch. Vast valleys were formed by the fat tyres, the soft earth being forced into peaks on either side of the wheels. The rain was beginning to ease off. Briella leaned forward and peered up through the windscreen. The sun would be shining before noon.

She glanced through the passenger window but was unable to see the sky. No way to tell if another system was building yet. The weather bureau had warned of dangerous weather over the next seven days, which, as far as Briella was concerned, was just perfect. Her sarcasm accelerator was set to full throttle. 'What more could go wrong than wonky magic and bad weather?' she thought before kicking herself for tempting the fates.

THE PUMPKIN PATCH

It had taken her and Scout over an hour to get back from the pumpkin patch. In her haste to get back there, Briella had forgotten to grab some supplies. Thirst and hunger would plague her long before nightfall and the air had already cooled from the rain. Her jumpsuit consisted of thinly woven fabric and would do little to keep out the cold air if a storm came through in the night.

Had she been human, she would have slapped her hand on the steering wheel in frustration. Something she had observed April doing on many occasions. As it was, she could do nothing else but hold onto the controller and operate the vehicle. She was afraid if she stamped her foot, it might go through the floor.

Her pinky finger tapped the underside of the device. It was a small action but enough to vent some of her annoyance. The path seemed to be a lot bumpier with herself at the controls. Perhaps that was because both her hands were now busy, and she wasn't able to hold on to the bars like before. This was what she allowed herself to believe, anyway. As you can imagine, the drive ended up being tiresome, lonely and painful.

When Briella arrived at her destination, she knew she had been right to come. Parking amongst the pumpkins was a terrifying thought but a necessary action. Past experience had taught her that children came out to play in the rain once the danger of lighting had passed. If they were to venture her way, she wanted to feel she had done everything she could to remain hidden.

With any luck, nobody would dare trespass on April and Force's new property, anyway. As far as the community was concerned, the property belonged to them already. They also believed April to be a federal agent and Force, a special investigator.

For now, Briella was pretty sure that Scout worried about these things for nothing. That might change when the Gatherers actually took ownership of the house and land. The townspeople liked the Gatherers, a lot.

Force and Scout, along with some of the local children, were instrumental in saving and returning the children captured by the Jealousy Monsters. April assisted in helping the children to overcome their feelings of jealousy and adjusting to normal life in society.

Force had a way of drawing children to him. It was like an instinctual attraction towards a protective force within the universe. That was also why Force and Scout had such a close relationship. She had a knack for sensing creatures that posed the greatest danger to children.

Briella took great comfort in Scout's abilities. If the pumpkins were a threat to the children of the town, Scout would have sensed it before they'd left the vegetable patch. The stirring to life would have already begun occurring to the pumpkin her fairy dust had blanketed. If it were to become dangerous like the pencil, surely Scout would know.

It didn't matter that the pumpkin was indigenous to Earth and that a Locator Fairy's senses only detected those creatures that were non-indigenous to the planet. Briella, also being a Locator Fairy, was well aware of this fact. Out of fear for what her magic was capable of at this time of the year, and awe over Scout's amazing abilities, she had attributed abilities to Scout that didn't exist.

"Scout will make everything okay. She knew how to deal with the pencil, zapping the magic right out of it. If the pumpkins have come to life, she will fix that, too. I will need to be very careful from now on to make sure that I don't get overexcited or scared until All Hallow's Eve has come to an end," she muttered to herself.

Briella wriggled out of the car, adding to the bumps and bruises she had already received from the pencil. There was no way she was ever going to be as graceful as Scout entering and exiting the vehicle.

Perhaps, April could work out a way to remove the doors and put them on hinges. Then she thought she might be better off asking Force. April was pretty protective of her helicopter. The Jeep probably wouldn't be any different.

Briella listened intently, ready to dive back through the window if there was any indication of trouble. Everything seemed in order. She gazed at the pumpkins attentively. Nothing appeared out of the ordinary.

The pumpkins were the same colour, the vines were still attached, and they were silent and motionless. Briella let out the breath she'd been holding and leaned against the jeep's door.

She placed her finger against the pulse point in her wrist. Her heart was beating a little fast but nothing to worry about. It would slow down now that she'd seen the pumpkins were inanimate with her own eyes.

Briella flapped her wings and grinned with relief, the rain had stopped. She flew to the roof and stood on the shade-clothed peaks, inspecting the landscape. From her new vantage point, she could see the small rises and falls that had sent her bouncing around the vehicle as she journeyed the countryside.

She could also see that the raised garden beds had an assortment of vegetables, capsicums, tomatoes, beans, carrots, lettuces, onions and strawberries. Then there were the cornfields, which looked even more impressive and terrifying, from this angle.

The cold from the cloth beneath her feet began to seep into her bones. She probably should have worn leather soled shoes rather than her high-heels with the thinner, plastic sole.

They were fashion statements, not practical footwear. Not ideal in a situation where hailstones that hadn't slid off the peaked roof littered her feet and were still the size of a pea. To a fairy, such as herself, the top of said pea came to ankle bone height.

She flew down to the pumpkin she had danced on and circled it from a distance. Once she was sure it was dormant, she landed on top and leaned against the vine stalk. Deciding the magic had worked on the pencil so early because of its small size, she stretched her hands above her head. "Dodged a bullet there," she laughed out loud.

Her blood ran cold as a nasally voice filled the quiet. "Who's there? Show yourself, you invisible ingrate. How dare you interrupt our peaceful afternoon!"

THE PUMPKIN PATCH

"Oh, brother!" she shivered, the vibrations from the pumpkin below being felt through her feet.

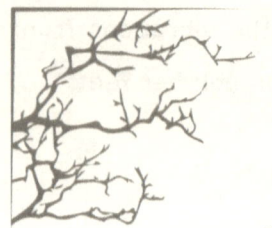

Chapter Thirteen

Briella slid down the vine until she hit the thicker part of the stalk. Her left arm lay on her knees, and her chin rested on her right fist. She had no idea how she was supposed to contain the situation. The pumpkin was so much bigger than her, and if others began to awaken, she would be outnumbered.

There had to be a reason for her magic to go haywire at this time of the year. No matter how far or wide she searched for answers, she hadn't been able to find any. The only comfort she could take from this situation was that this very scenario had happened once before, many years ago.

If these pumpkins were anything like the last lot, all she had to do was keep them arguing among themselves. While they were fighting with one another, they were not thinking of other ways to cause trouble, or discovering they were able to move about. Briella took a deep breath, picked herself up and flew down to face the pumpkin.

The pumpkin was scarier than the previous pumpkins had been. The eyes were huge and irate looking, lit within by a bright green light. The eyebrows followed the shape of its eyes adding another layer of scary to the horror of its face. The mouth turned up at the edges and had vertical lines similar in appearance to stitches at regular intervals along its length. "What are you looking at, Flutterbug?" it growled.

"You are a pumpkin that has come to life by fairy dust," she replied.

"Is that so?" it asked.

"Yes. Do you feel strange in any way?"

"How would I know?" it growled in reply. "What have I got to compare my feelings to?"

"Well do you hurt or tingle anywhere?"

"I don't even understand what that is. Why are you here? Why don't you go away?"

"I am responsible for you," she shrugged.

"You are responsible for nobody but yourself. Why would you say such a thing?"

93

"Because I created you," she stated.

"Even so, you cannot control the thoughts or actions of others, even me. Now go away. I want to be alone."

"Then get lost," another voice piped into the conversation.

"Oh no," Briella cried, glancing behind her to see another pair of eyes glaring at her. They reminded her of flames, flickers branching off at the top and glowing like a pair of suns. The mouth reminded her of the teeth on a saw, jagged and sharp.

"This is my patch of land. I was here first. You get lost."

"Can't get lost if I can see where I'm going and remember where I've been," the new pumpkin replied. Briella flicked her head from one to the other. It was going to get confusing if she didn't come up with names for them both. She turned to the one who spoke first and said, "You are going to be referred to as P-One."

"I am not being named after them little . . ."

"Careful," she warned.

94

THE PUMPKIN PATCH

"What? Those little cretins already think they are better than us. Sprouting off about being a 'green' vegetable. No way am I going to let you make them worse by allowing them to believe we have been named in their honour."

"Fine, then I'll call you Jack."

"I don't want to be called Jack."

"Why not?"

"I don't like that word, and I won't answer to it!" he stormed.

"How should I get your attention then? Hey, you?"

"Definitely not!" he shouted, lifting slightly off the ground. He was so riled by her words that he hadn't even noticed. The other pumpkin had, however. "You will refer to me as John."

"John?" she wrinkled her nose, "Why John?"

"I like the way it sounds, smooth like me."

"Fine," she turned her attention to the other pumpkin. "You can be called Jack."

"I ain't taking nobody's seconds. I am not going to be called Jack, either."

John's voice rumbled in a deep chuckle. So much so, that the air around her vibrated a little like

95

thunder in a storm. "Be quiet, John. Well, what do you want to be called then?"

"Hmm, Late For Dinner," he answered with a smirk.

"I am not calling you that. What a ridiculous name."

"'Tis not. Humans say that a lot."

"Late for dinner?"

"Yep," he tipped himself up slightly, similar to when a person lifted their chin. "They say you can call me whatever you want, just don't call me late for dinner. So, I think that is the perfect name. Late For Dinner."

"She should call you Whacko," John replied. "You should humour him. None of us will."

"You've got that right," a female voice piped up.

"Good Lord," Briella groaned. She glanced over to see a pumpkin with sky blue eyes squinting at her and a mouth large enough to be able to swallow her whole. She turned and glared at John.

"What?" his demeanour swiftly changed to one of innocence. Briella narrowed her eyes. She might have brought him to life, but the animation of the others was all on him.

"And who might you be?" Briella asked, keeping her gaze on John.

"I don't know. Who am I?" The pumpkin replied with a confused tone.

"What do you want to be known as?" Briella asked, taking her eyes off John and flying over to her.

"What would be a good name?" she replied.

"How about Pumpkinita?"

"Ooh, that sounds pretty. What is your name?"

Briella blinked. None of the others had thought to ask.

"Briella."

"Both our names end in 'a'. Did you do that on purpose?"

"I hadn't really thought about it," Briella confessed. She had merely added 'ita' to the end of pumpkin to make it sound more feminine.

"Well I think it was very clever of you to come up with matching names," Pumpkinita stated with a grin that made her appear hungry. Briella managed to suppress the shiver that threatened to shake her body. So far, that pumpkin had been friendly, and she didn't want to do anything to change that.

"Looks like we got a suck-up, John. What do you think we should do with her?"

"Pumpkin pie, scones, soup. Oh, so many selections to choose from."

"Looks like she's got enough weight on her to manage all three," Late For Dinner said nastily.

"Okay, that's enough!" Briella said crossly.

"Thank you, Briella," Pumpkinita replied.

"Says the pet of the flutterbug," John snarled.

"Somebody's jealous," a young soprano stated.

"Really, John. How many more are going to come alive?"

John's consciousness followed the vine attached to his head. "That should be the last of them. Only three others have sprouted from this vine."

"Do you have any other vines attached to yours?"

"Nope, do you think I'm nuts or something?"

"Nobody said anything about nuts," the newbie sang. "She's been talking about pumpkins or haven't you been listening."

THE PUMPKIN PATCH

"Your name is?" Briella asked the newcomer.

"Tunes."

"Welcome to the conscious state of the pumpkin patch."

"You didn't welcome me," Pumpkinita said sadly, spinning away from Briella.

Briella wondered if it wouldn't be better for her sanity to leave them to it. What harm could they do to anyone, really?

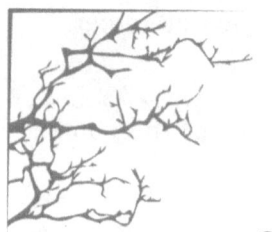

Chapter Fourteen

Briella managed to smooth over Pumpkinita's hurt feelings, bringing the ratio of good pumpkins versus nasty back to square. She spent most of her time conversing with Pumpkinita and Tunes, doing her best to ignore John and Late For Dinner as much as possible.

However, after half an hour, Pumpkinita and Tunes began to turn snarky. The other two were utterly insufferable, and Briella was at the point of tearing her hair out. "I can't do this!" she yelled, then broke into heartfelt sobs. "I work my guts out each year keeping the humans safe and then Halloween rocks around, and I do something to threaten them myself."

"What are you talking about, Miss Sooky Pants?" John grumbled.

"Nothing. I was muttering to myself, and it is none of your business anyway."

"It is our business," John and Late For Dinner stated simultaneously. With a growl of warning, John continued while Late For Dinner kept his mouth closed. "Did you or did you not imply that we are a threat to humanity?"

"Yes. You are inanimate objects that have been animated by fairy dust. I told you that before."

"So, that makes us a threat to humanity?"

"Well, doesn't it?"

"No! We just want to live peacefully in our pumpkin patch without a noisy sooky pants blabbering away."

"Speak for yourself, John. I want a body to attach to this handsome head of mine. I don't want to be stuck here forever, listening to you lot griping at each other. I want to be free to roam and see the world."

"That's a great idea, L.F.D. Briella should hook us up with some legs since she is responsible for creating us in the first place," Pumpkinita suggested.

"Nah, uh," Briella shook her head. "I am responsible for bringing John to life, not you or the other two. That is all on him."

"Then you should get John a body, and he can fix us up with one," Pumpkinita said.

"Don't you start, too" Briella whined.

"Why not? There is nothing wrong with wanting to improve one's quality of life."

"You are only alive until sunrise tomorrow," Briella advised.

"Are you going to kill us, chop us up, and eat us?" Tunes chorused in, horrified by the thought.

"No, you will just go back to what you were before," she said.

"Weren't we alive before?"

"Technically, yes."

"Then why did you say we would only be alive until tomorrow morning?" Tunes was quite confused.

"Because you won't be able to talk afterwards like you are now."

"But we will still be alive?" she asked again.

"Yes, Tunes. You will still be alive."

"Then like the others said, we will need to be given legs at the very least."

Briella raised her face to the ceiling, "Lord, give me strength."

"You can have some of mine." Late For Dinner tipped sideways, startling himself. He rolled for a few seconds then whooped with happiness. After seeing John jump earlier, it had only been a matter of time before he worked out how to move himself. He rocked himself until he was up on his side again. The extra burst of energy enabled him to roll further. If he could only work out how to control his movement so that he didn't overbalance. Late For Dinner had somehow ended up upside down.

Pumpkinita bounced on the spot, much to Briella's horror. "How did you do that?" she demanded, moving closer to Late For Dinner's original position.

"With a lot less energy than you are expending to be able to move. You've got to tip yourself slightly then let gravity take over."

"That doesn't make sense. I don't understand what to do," she wailed.

"Actually, I discovered this by accident. Keep trying until you get the same result as me. Remember what you did then repeat the process."

"So we don't need legs?" Tunes sang.

"Not to get around with. Arms wouldn't hurt, though. Imagine what we could do with a pair of those."

"You need to stay here," Briella said, her voice wobbled with panic.

"Why? Because you said?" John scoffed. "If they want to go, let them go. Seriously, Flutterbug, how much trouble can they get up to in less than a day?"

Briella flinched. Those words were eerily similar to her own thoughts. She couldn't let them have their freedom. There was the chance they would be spotted by the humans. "I'm sorry, John. It's just not possible for them to leave the pumpkin patch."

His face screwed up as though in pain. She fluttered closer, placing her hand against his cheek. "I know you have asked for peace and quiet. You will have that again tomorrow morning."

"No, I will have it sooner than you think," he whispered, careful not to blow her away. Briella glanced around to see that she and John were the only two left in the vicinity. The other pumpkins had rolled away.

"What happened to your tether?"

"Late For Dinner snapped it."

"Where are they?"

"I don't know. I can't feel them anymore," he admitted.

Briella was at a loss what to do. "Will they be together?"

"Hard to say," John answered. He viewed her indecisiveness with great interest. "You seem to have a dilemma. You can leave to find them and try to bring them back, or you can stay here with me and let them run amok in your town. Hmmm, what to do?"

Briella glared at him. When this was over, she was going to tie her hands behind her back and stay away from any influence that could get the production of fairy dust kicking along. "I don't really have a choice, do I? There's three of them, and one of you."

"Damn straight. Don't worry, Flutterbug, I'll still be here when you get back."

"My name is Briella."

"I know. Flutterbug suits you better. Now go on, those pumpkins won't come back on their own." Briella hesitated and received a gentle nudge from John. She flew up onto the roof to get a better vantage point. She spotted Tunes first and took off after her.

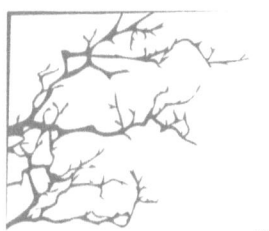

Chapter Fifteen

Tunes was fast. Really fast. Lucky for humans their young didn't pick up the knack of crawling and walking as quickly as that pumpkin had learnt how to roll.

Briella put her head down and flew as swiftly as she could manage. Once she'd caught up with Tunes, she tried to reason with her. When that didn't work, Briella lined up a flight path to take that pumpkin down.

"You can do this," Briella muttered before putting herself into a spiralling descent. Hands held in a diving position, she lifted her head at the last minute and flattened her palms in front of her. Pulling herself out of a spin, she hit Tunes with a force that threatened to shatter the bones in her body. Tunes stopped rolling on her side and began tumbling top over tail.

"Ahhhhh!" Tune's screams filled the air. "I'm crashing. Help!"

Briella worried that she would discover Tunes bruised beyond repair. She didn't mean to be that rough in her approach. The goal was to put Tunes on her butt. When Tunes came to a stop, Briella found a couple of scratches on her skin. Other than that, she appeared to be okay.

"And you say we are dangerous," Tunes pouted. "You're a nasty piece of work, Fairy."

"That may be the case, but it doesn't change the fact that you are a Very. Naughty. Pumpkin. Now, roll yourself back to the pumpkin patch."

"I don't think so," she stated, her tone filled with attitude.

"John has a surprise for you."

"Then he can give it to me later. I'm busy."

"Doing what?" Briella looked for something that would offer her some assistance in getting Tunes back to her home. She was annoyed to find nothing of help in the area.

"Living," Tunes replied.

THE PUMPKIN PATCH

Briella thought back to the last time this happened but realised that wouldn't help her under these circumstances. The pumpkins that came alive during a previous mishap of magic were contained in a transport vehicle on their way to market.

By the time the farmers sold most of the first truckload and began unpacking the second, the sun had come up, freezing the grumbling pumpkins' poses into place. At that time, the popularity of the jack-o-lantern hadn't taken off, but stories of pumpkins with scary faces being seen on Halloween were passed around, leading to the commercialisation of them today.

Her previous mishap did offer up an idea, though. If she could gather the pumpkins and place them in some sort of containment device until morning, her problem would be solved. Comparing the size of Tunes to herself, she wasn't sure how she was going to overpower the resistant vegetable.

The soprano began rocking onto her side. Briella gave another push, but the pumpkin was ready this time. Tunes pushed back, getting up on her side, allowing the slight fall in the ground level to help her get rolling.

Briella's frustration gauge was nearing its limit. She would either scream until her voice became hoarse, or cry a river of tears. At this point, Briella didn't know which way the pendulum was going to swing. She just knew she was headed for trouble.

"There has to be something I can use," she growled, engrossed in her search. A yelp turned her head in the direction of an approaching dog as her wings carried her higher to safety. At first, she felt surprised at not having picked up on the sound of it panting. When she realised who it was, a burst of happiness filled her, "You little ripper!"

Scout was riding on the back of a red and white husky. The fur on his neck held tightly in her hands. His tongue lolled to the left, a grin stretched across his face. Apparently, the husky and Scout had a trusting relationship. She wondered where they'd met, then his eyes captured her attention. "Really, Liam," Briella said, throwing her hands in the air. Only he would not have the sense to change the colour of his eyes from coral to that of a real dog.

THE PUMPKIN PATCH

She returned her focus to Scout. The grin on her face was highly infectious. Briella found herself smiling in return. "Thank the Gods you are both here. I have caused a situation that I could use a hand to rectify."

"I figured something was wrong when you took off so fast. You should have told me what was going on instead of trying to deal with it on your own."

"I know. I didn't want to worry you on a hunch. I wasn't sure there was an issue until I arrived and discovered the pumpkins were coming to life."

'I think you need to tell me what is going on,' Force said through mind-link.

"Later," Scout replied. "We need to deal with this first. How many are we talking about?"

"Four. But only three have taken off. The first to become animated has agreed to stay at the pumpkin patch."

"And you believed it?" Scout asked, eyebrows raised with a higher pitch to her voice.

"Not really, but what choice did I have? Stay with him or round up the other three. What would you have done?"

"Rounded up the other three," Scout agreed. "How can we help?"

"I think if we can get them back to the pumpkin patch and pen them in somehow, our worries will be over."

'That will be an easier task once I am in human form,' Force stated through mind-link. 'I'll need you to dismount first, Scout.'

The transformation was swift. His light brown hair was shaped into a buzz cut style, and his strong jawline was clenched tight. His button-up shirt was a stormy grey, and his jeans were stone-wash blue. His feet were protected by steel-capped boots.

Briella looked him over, appreciating the view. "You look hotter than a frying pan, Liam."

Scout had to agree. She thought he was gorgeous in the singlet tops he wore that allowed the onlooker to appreciate his muscular arms. Having them hidden by the sleeves of his shirt made the imagination run wilder.

"Which way did they go?"

"Tunes went that way," Briella pointed into the distance where they could barely make out the outline of the pumpkin's shape. "I haven't got a clue where to start looking for the others," she shrugged.

Force came up with a plan, "I'll go get that one and bring it back. You two find the location of the others and try to keep them stationary."

"Okay." Briella and Scout saluted him. Force transformed back into the form of the husky and bounded after Tunes. Scout and Briella headed back to the pumpkin patch. Scout landed on the roof and surveyed the landscape while Briella checked on John before joining her.

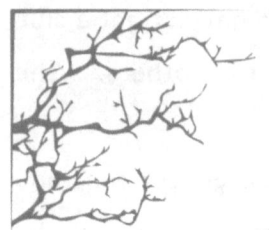

Chapter Sixteen

"I'm really sorry, Scout."

"Don't sweat it, Briella. Over there," she pointed to the left, "headed for the house."

"I see it," Briella responded, flapping her wings and rising off the shade-cloth. "Should we go together or do you want to try to find the other one."

"I think we should separate."

"Okay, but you should know, they are quite nasty."

"I can handle a few snarky remarks. Do they bite?"

"Not yet."

"Don't forget to tell Liam where I am."

"I won't." Scout watched her fly away then continued looking for the third, unable to pinpoint its location. She could fly around and hope to stumble across it, or she could wait for Force to return. He could turn into a giant bird of prey and cover more airspace in a few seconds than she could in minutes.

Scout only had to wait a few minutes before she spotted him running in her direction, pumpkin held securely under his arm. As he got closer, she could hear Tunes singing in protest. "Help, Help, I'm being abducted."

"Pipe down, or I will squash you." She heard Force reply.

"I will not become a squash. They are squishy and icky," she sang.

"I didn't say you would become . . ., never mind."

Scout flew down to greet him. "You got it."

"I am not an 'it'. I am a female."

"Good for you," Scout replied. "How are you going to contain it while we capture the others?"

Forced glanced around looking for something to hold the pumpkin in place. He spotted some thinner vines hanging from the primary, thicker vine that had tethered them to one another. "I could thread this between her eyes and mouth, wrapping it around the post over there. If she takes off again, it will rip a hole in the remaining flesh."

"That won't stop her from trying to escape. I doubt that would even cause her pain."

"How do you propose we contain her?"

Scout tapped her cheek with a pointer finger while she considered their options. "Why don't we create a triangular pen with some of the shade-cloth from the roof? We could place the pumpkins inside, and they wouldn't be able to escape."

"What if we just wrapped the four of them inside the shade-cloth instead of making a pen?" Force countered.

"I am not going in there with them," John shouted, but was overridden by Tune's lovely voice.

"Oh, please don't do that," Tune's vibrato was exquisite. "I'm afraid of the dark and confined spaces."

"How would you know?" Scout frowned.

"I just do," she whined.

"Fine, we'll run with your idea, Scout," he said as he began dismantling part of the ceiling.

"Oh thank you, kind sir," Tunes ended with a crescendo.

"Why don't you start looking for another pumpkin?" Force asked Scout.

"It will be quicker if I help you do this and then ride on the back of an eagle. Briella has gone after the second, but I wasn't able to locate the third. Together, we should be able to spot it in no time."

"Sounds like a plan," he grinned, eager to take to the skies.

Force wrapped the length of cloth around three of the posts then used his control over the element of fire to pull some static electricity from the air and generate some heat. This enabled him to seal the edges together and secure the enclosure. John and Tunes were picked up and placed inside.

"You're going to pay for this," her high pitched threat had them placing their hands over their ears in pain. John remained unusually quiet.

"Let's go. We should probably help Briella before chasing down the third pumpkin if we can find it."

"I agree." He transformed into a magnificent bird, spreading his wings while waiting for Scout to get settled. He ran along the ground until he got lift then flew into the air, reverting to mind-link to continue their conversation. *'Briella seemed quite stressed earlier. The least amount of time she has to manage on her own, the better.'*

Neither of them could see where Pumpkinita had disappeared to. They could see the pumpkin that Briella had gone after bouncing up and down on the spot. Someone wasn't happy. Scout marvelled at Briella's ability to keep him from moving further away. She was pretty sure that if the tables were turned, that pumpkin would still be rolling away from her, laughing with glee.

Rather than landing, Force grasped the pumpkin with his talons then circled above until Briella climbed on board, before returning to the pumpkin patch. Late For Dinner closed his eyes, screaming with fear. "Don't drop me," he cried, imagining himself smashing open on impact with the ground.

"We are not going to drop you," Scout assured him. Force lowered him gently to the ground and hopped a couple of times before remaining motionless. Scout and Briella flew off so that he could morph back and place the pumpkin in his new pen.

"Did you find, Pumpkinita?"

"No, we couldn't spot it anywhere," Scout answered.

"What are we going to do?"

"Let me out, let me out!" Late For Dinner chanted.

"If you don't shut your mouth I will kick you out," Tunes replied.

"You can't kick me out because you don't have any legs," Late For Dinner said.

"Only because John hasn't found us any, yet. But when he does . . ."

"Do you think you could wrap some of that stuff around their mouths to keep them quiet?" John asked.

"Stuff it," Late For Dinner responded.

"That would be even better," John chuckled.

Force turned to Briella, "Are you going to tell me how this came about?"

Briella shook her head, "We still haven't found, Pumpkinita. She could be anywhere."

A scream that gauged the same response as fingernails down the blackboard came from the wooded area behind them. They all spun around to see Pumpkinita speeding towards them with a giant hare right behind her. "Briella, save me! She wants to eat me."

Force morphed into the husky and bounded towards the hare. Its eyes widened in fear as it turned tail and ran. Pumpkinita rolled right up to the fairies and said, "Hold me."

"Don't be ridiculous," John growled. "Look at the size of them."

Force returned and placed Pumpkinita in the enclosure. "Now will you tell me what is going on?"

"Sure. Why not?" Briella sighed. She told him about the troubles she had with magic at this time of year. Scout informed him she had made a suggestion that Briella refrained from using her magic until Halloween had passed.

"That sounds like a good idea," Force nodded.

"So what did you get up to this morning?" Scout asked, taking the focus off Briella. "You were gone very early."

"I had some stuff to do in the city," he replied.

"What kind of stuff?" her voice grew sweeter than usual.

Force knew that tone. She would continue to bring the conversation back to that topic until she had an answer. So he told the truth. "I bought you and Briella a gift for the fairy garden."

"You did?" they chorused.

"Yes. You're not getting it until settlement day, so don't keep harping on it."

Scout appeared very satisfied. "I told you I would find out where he'd gone," she whispered out of the corner of her mouth. Force, as usual, pretended not to hear.

Briella copied her mode of speaking, "Do you think you can find out what it is?"

"Yes, but I don't want to. I am looking forward to settlement day even more now."

Briella thought about it. "Me too," she decided.

"What should we do now?" Force asked.

"You and Scout can go home if you like. I'm going to wait until morning to make sure the pumpkins return to their natural state."

"We will wait with you," Force said.

"You don't have to."

"We know," Scout replied, making herself comfortable on top of John's head.

"Don't go sitting on top of me, Flutterbug."

"But you're my favourite."

That statement began a pumpkin argument that lasted for the rest of the afternoon and well into the night. Force left them for an hour to get some supplies, returning with April.

Force and April built a fire and toasted some bread, piling warmed baked beans and spaghetti on top. Dessert consisted of toasted marshmallows with hot chocolate. Scout and Briella feasted on mushrooms and daisy nectar.

Everyone had an enjoyable night. Even the pumpkins joined in for a campfire sing-along and ghost stories. As the night wore on, they ran out of songs to sing and things to say, causing long bouts of silence.

Then, just before sunrise, Briella made a remark that put a fire under the pumpkins again. "I think I might take you home with me, John, as a remembrance of this night." As the sun peeked above the horizon, the flesh of the pumpkins hardened, sealing their angry expressions forever.

"Our very own Halloween jack-o-lanterns," Briella stated proudly, now that the magic had dissipated and the danger had disappeared.

The group packed up their stuff and headed back to the pub. "I'm glad that's over," Briella breathed with relief. Force and April agreed. Scout couldn't bring herself to acknowledge the remark and kept her mouth shut. She had a niggling feeling that their troubles had only just begun.

Titles by Marnie Atwell

Starlight Investigations

Jealousy Monsters

Vampire

Phantasm

Halloween Madness

The Pumpkin Patch

The House of Horrors

The Spirited Scarecrow

The Curious Kitten

About the Author

Marnie is an Australian author who lives in South-East Queensland with her husband and two children. When she is not dreaming up new adventures for her characters; Marnie enjoys writing, reading paranormal romance novels, and spending time with her family and friends. Not necessarily in that order.

Visit her website at: www.marnieatwell.com for more books, pictures, and downloads.

The next book in this series is:

The House of Horrors